The Lady with the Alligator Purse

Repeat this melody for each verse in the song.

Key of G

Miss Lu - cy had a ba - by, His name was Ti - ny Tim, She

put him in the bath - tub____ to see if he could swim. He

drank up all the wa - ter, He ate up all the soap, He

tried to eat the bath - tub, but it would - n't go down his throat.

Little, Brown and Company

Hachette Book Group
237 Park Avenue, New York, NY 10017
Visit our website at www.lb-kids.com

Little, Brown and Company is a division of Hachette Book Group, Inc.
The Little, Brown name and logo are trademarks of Hachette Book Group, Inc.

First Board Book Edition: April 1998
First Paperback Edition: September 1990
Originally published in hardcover in 1988 by Little, Brown and Company

The Sing-Along Stories name and logo are trademarks of Hachette Book Group, Inc.

Library of Congress Cataloging-in-Publication Data

Westcott, Nadine Bernard.
     The lady with the alligator purse.
     Summary: The old jump rope/nonsense rhyme features an ailing young Tiny Tim.
     ISBN 978-0-316-93136-6
1. Jump rope rhymes. 2. Nonsense verses. 3. Children's poetry. [1. Jump rope rhymes.
2. Nonsense verses.] I. Title.
PZ8.3.W4998Lad 1998   87-21368

PB: 30 29 28 27 26 25
SC

Manufactured in China

The illustrations for this book were done in watercolor and ink.
The text was set in Cheltenham, and the display type is Fontoon.

The Lady with the Alligator Purse

Adapted and illustrated by

Nadine Bernard Westcott

Series Editor, Mary Ann Hoberman

Megan Tingley Books

LITTLE, BROWN AND COMPANY
New York   Boston

For
Jim and Sandy
Love, Deanie

Miss Lucy had a baby,
His name was Tiny Tim,

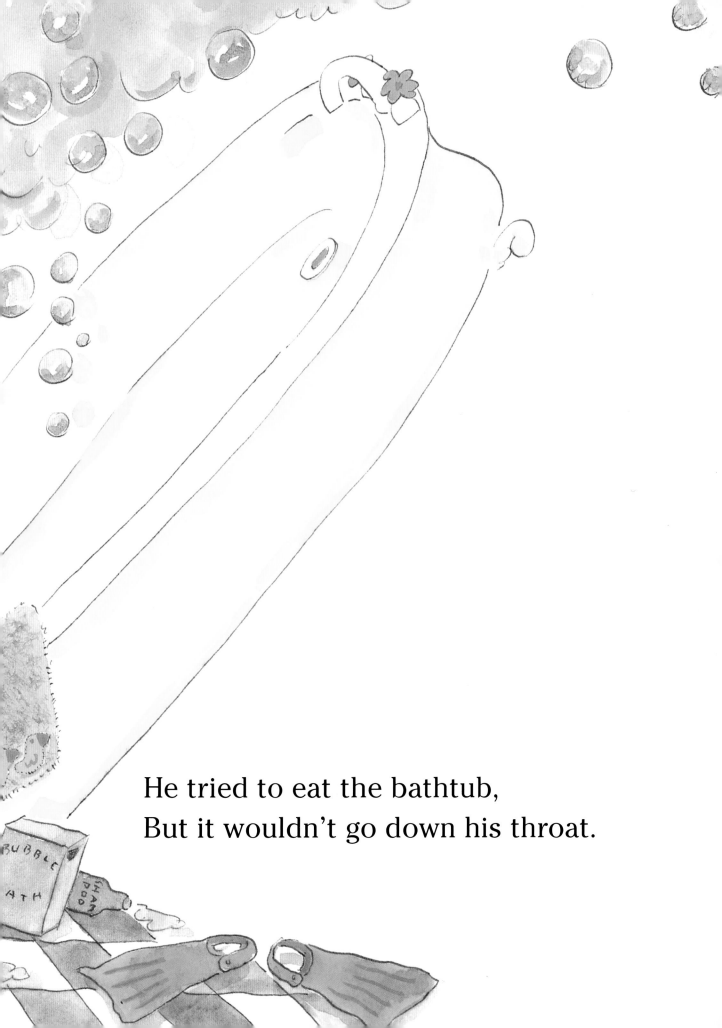

He tried to eat the bathtub,
But it wouldn't go down his throat.

Miss Lucy called the doctor,

Miss Lucy called the nurse,

Miss Lucy called the lady
With the alligator purse.

In came the doctor,
In came the nurse,
In came the lady
With the alligator purse.

"Mumps," said the doctor,

"Measles," said the nurse,

"Nonsense!" said the lady
With the alligator purse.

"Penicillin," said the doctor,

"Castor oil," said the nurse,

"Pizza!" said the lady
With the alligator purse.

Out went the doctor,
Out went the nurse,

Out went the lady
With the alligator purse.

More fun with *The Lady with the Alligator Purse*!

❶ Look at the second and third pages where Miss Lucy puts Tiny Tim in the bathtub to see if he can swim. Name the items in the picture that are probably too large to use in the bathtub. Where else could Tiny Tim play with some of these items? Draw a picture of Tiny Tim using some of them in a different place.

❷ The doctor thinks that Tiny Tim has the mumps. The nurse thinks that he has the measles. Find out what Tiny Tim would look like if he had the mumps or the measles. What do you think is wrong with him?

❸ Name the different toppings that can be on a pizza. Make a pizza out of construction paper, using appropriate colors and shapes to represent your favorite toppings. Divide the pizza into slices to share with family, friends, or classmates. How many slices can you each have?

❹ Suppose the lady with the alligator purse has a collection of purses that represent different animals. Design a new animal purse for her.

❺ Find pairs of rhyming words in the song (for example, "Tim" and "swim"). Can you think of other words that rhyme with these pairs?

Activities prepared by Pat Scales, Director of Library Services, South Carolina Governor's School for the Arts and Humanities, Greenville, SC.